grade 3

GW00370878

For full details of exam requirements, please refer to the current syllabus in conjunction with *Examination Information & Regulations* and the guide for candidates, teachers and parents, *These Music Exams*. These three documents are available online at www.abrsm.org, as well as free of charge from music retailers, from ABRSM local representatives or from the Services Department, The Associated Board of the Royal Schools of Music, 24 Portland Place, London W1B 1LU, United Kingdom.

CONTENTS

In this album, editorial additions to the texts are given in small print, within square brackets, or – in the case of slurs and ties – in the form ⌒. Metronome marks, breath marks (retained here where they appear in the source edition) and ornament realizations (suggested for exam purposes) are for guidance only; they are not comprehensive or obligatory.

Footnotes: Anthony Burton

DO NOT PHOTOCOPY © MUSIC

Alternative pieces for this grade

Music origination by Barnes Music Engraving Ltd
Cover by Økvik Design
Printed in England by Halstan & Co. Ltd, Amersham, Bucks.

Menuet

BWV Anh. II 115

from *Clavierbüchlein vor Anna Magdalena Bach, 1725*

Arranged by
Howard Harrison

12·10·11

PEZOLD

The 'Little Book of Keyboard Pieces' which Johann Sebastian Bach compiled in 1725 for his second wife, Anna Magdalena, consists largely of music by composers other than himself. One of them is this Menuet (originally one of a pair), long attributed to Bach, but now known to be a movement from a suite by the Dresden organist Christian Pezold (1677–1733).

Witches' Dance

A:2

Arranged by
Paul Harris and Emma Johnson

T. KULLAK

Theodor Kullak (1818–82) was a celebrated pianist and piano teacher in 19th-century Germany. He published more than 100 original works and sets of pieces, mostly for solo piano – the original medium of this *Witches' Dance*.

Melody

from *Méthode complète de clarinette*

Arranged by
Paul Harris

BERR

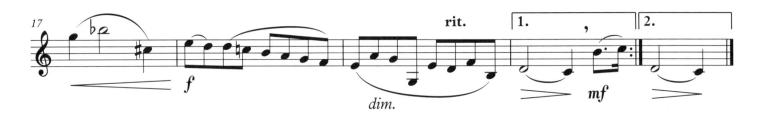

Friedrich Berr (1794–1838) was born in the German town of Mannheim, but spent most of his career in Paris as an orchestral performer and teacher. He made some well-known arrangements for wind quartet of Rossini's early string sonatas, and himself composed numerous clarinet pieces and a *Complete Method for Clarinet*. 'Melody' is one of 21 studies in phrasing in this tutor; it was originally a clarinet duet, but it is printed here in an arrangement with piano.

Carol

No. 3 from *Five Bagatelles*

B:1

FINZI

Gerald Finzi (1901–56) was one of the leading British composers of the generation after Vaughan Williams and Holst. He composed very slowly and self-critically, and clarinettists are lucky to have both his Concerto with string orchestra and his set of *Five Bagatelles* with piano – the latter completed in 1943, and including this 'Carol'.

B:2

Jazz Three

No. 15 from *Rhythm & Rag for Clarinet*

ALAN HAUGHTON

Alan Haughton (b. 1950) studied piano at the Royal Academy of Music, where he became interested in jazz. He has written many pieces for young performers, including the *Rhythm & Rag* series for various instruments. This waltz is jazzy not only in its syncopated rhythms but also in some of its harmonies.

Reproduced from Alan Haughton: *Rhythm & Rag for Clarinet* (ABRSM Publishing)

AB 3349

A Hungarian Tale

B:3

CHRISTOPHER GUNNING

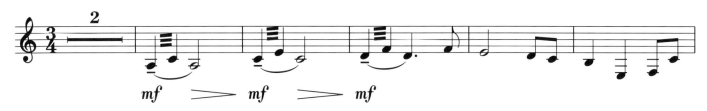

Christopher Gunning (b. 1944) is best known as an award-winning composer for film and television – notably for *Agatha Christie's Poirot*. But he has also written educational music, including several pieces for the clarinet collection *Going Solo*. This one is given a 'Hungarian' feeling by the use of tremolos to suggest the cimbalom of Hungarian folk music.

C:1

Study in C
from *Elementarschule für Klarinette*

DEMNITZ

Elementarschule für Klarinette Elementary School for Clarinet

The German clarinettist Friedrich Demnitz (1845–90) studied at the Dresden Conservatoire, and later taught there, while also playing as principal clarinettist in the city's court orchestra. This study from his *Elementary School for Clarinet* is the first of a group concentrating on scales.

Strange, but True

No. 8 from *Style Workout for Solo Clarinet*

C:2

JAMES RAE

James Rae (b. 1957) is a clarinettist and saxophonist, a teacher, and the composer of a great deal of educational wind music. This study comes from the 'classical' section of a collection of 40 studies intended to enable players to become 'conversant with all styles of music'. The composer advises that you should 'play this with great flexibility and always aim to shape the phrases well'.

C:3

Shanty
from *A Miscellany for Clarinet*, Book 2

MICHAEL ROSE

Michael Rose, OBE (b. 1934) is a well-known conductor and composer of music for young players; he has conducted the Bedfordshire County Youth Orchestra for many years. This piece comes from a collection of clarinet pieces exploring a variety of moods and styles. A shanty is a sea song, originally sung by sailors as they worked at a task requiring a regular rhythm.